A Story From

Gnome Hollow

Legend of The "Mono Gnome"

Written and illustrated by "Little John" Adams

WestBow Press books may be ordered through booksellers or by contacting:

WestBow Press
ɩ Oɩ ɩ noᴍᵉ ᴄison
ᴄᴏ ᴇᴍᴀᵉy Drive
Bloomington, IN 47403
www.westbowpress.com
1-(866) 928-1240

ISBN: 978-1-4497-9816-1 (sc)
ISBN: 978-1-4497-9817-8 (e)

Library of Congress Control Number: 2013910744

Printed in the United States of America.

WestBow Press rev. date: 7/23/2013

WestBow
PRESS
A DIVISION OF THOMAS NELSON

As the sun set behind the mountains, the night became unusually still. The full moon arched across the lake and glistened like diamonds. Beautiful yet strange this night was. Often, when I could not sleep, I would get up, go outside into the fresh air and ponder the gazillion stars overhead. I think most people's imagination comes alive when one walks in the dark. It's my favorite time to walk. As I meandered slowly along the shore

Just before sunset on Mono Lake

of the great and ancient Mono Lake, something distracted the corner of my eye. I saw what looked to be a very small person running through the tufa forest just ahead of me.

Tufa Towers

Now tufa, (pronounced toofa, for those who don't know) are stalagmite looking oddities that grow from the ground up. Some are as high as three or four of me standing on top of each other. They are made of calcium carbonate deposits, off-white in color, and are formed under water by the mixing of fresh water springs and minerals in the lake. It took a long period of time for tufa to be formed. Then, as the lake water receded, it left these magnificent structures exposed for all to see. Have you ever taken wet sand at the ocean and poured the ooze from your hand to let it plop onto itself? That plopping makes wonderfully unique sand castles. Well, that's what these tufa look like; only much, much bigger.

Moffee Vicket and his home

So, back to the story. I quickly followed this little person but could not keep up. Startling me, he suddenly jumped from behind a tufa smack dab in my path. My heart raced considerably, for I had never seen any living thing that looked quite like him.

When I was a child, my father told me of a gnome that lived on the shores of Mono Lake. He was so convincing that I absolutely believed his story. I suppose it's easier to believe parent trickery at an innocent and naïve young age. As I grew older, my belief in his story gave way to grown up pride and rational. I concluded my father was just a great story teller. I will always love his stories.

The little fellow standing in front of me smiled, extended his rather large hand and said, "Hi John. I'm Moffee, Moffee Vicket." An unusual name I thought, but the question was, how did he know my name? He invited me to his home which was incredibly crafted inside one of the tufa towers. I started wondering if this was truly happening. Was my mind playing tricks on me? I felt as though I was having a most pleasant dream, yet fully awake. At times when I looked at Moffee, it seemed as though he was taller or shorter than at other times. He would appear to be from one foot in height to perhaps three and a half feet at most; but always proportionate for the situation. He was very pudgy and had a comforting and disarming countenance about him. Even though I didn't speak my thoughts out loud, Moffee turned toward me and said, "Gnomes are suppose to be pudgy." And he laughed. He frequently twirled his pointer fingers through the mustache part of his magnificent beard. His cheeks were the color of a bright sierra wave sunset. After very little conversation, one could tell he was quite serious about the enjoyment of life. His carefree yet responsible spirit greatly intrigued me.

Cozy fireplace and soft sofa room

Once inside his tufa home, I had a strong desire to snooze by his fireplace. His home was so cozy and enticingly comfortable. I think I placed my hand on every polished river rock of his beautifully constructed fireplace. Each stone was a different earth tone color with what looked like a large gold nugget set high toward the top. A grand oak mantle graced his fireplace with pictures of what I presumed was his family and friends. Inside the fireplace was a large iron hook with a medium sized kettle hanging from it. From the kettle came the sweet aroma of blackberry tea, except of course during the Christmas season when it was full of Moffee's personal recipe of hot cider. Apparently it was a favorite among his many guests; I was told. On the hardwood floor, adorning each side of the fireplace, were two large vases with hand painted glazes encompassing the girth. Moffee said that I would be introduced to the vases soon enough. I didn't know exactly what he meant, but there was something exciting about it.

There was a combination cooking and dining area. In the center of the dining section was the most elegant oak table, which seemed to beckon all to come, sit, and break bread. Each leg of the table was masterfully hand carved with a bust that looked like it could be an elder of gnomes. On the sides of the table were sculpted reliefs of what appeared to be the north wind. As I rubbed my hand across the table, Moffee said to me "In the winter season, I very much

Moffee's brewing kettle

3

enjoy cross country skiing with the north wind caressing my face. The cold wind makes me feel alive and therefore blessed." From his cupboard, he grabbed a box of cornstarch, squeezed it and said "doesn't that sound just like walking in fresh snow?" I had to laugh, for indeed it did.

Skiing into the North Wind

Between the dining area and the large living room was a log beam archway exquisitely carved. It looked like something found in an English castle but on a smaller scale. The living room, called a soft sofa room by Moffee, had several overstuffed chairs and sofas. Many colorful pillows lay everywhere. There were big ones and little ones, of every shape and degree of comfort. Beneath it all was a soft, thick, braided rug, rich in color and most soothing to a weary foot. Graced on one of the walls, above one of the sofas was a stained glass window that would make a church envious.

Pillows of many shapes

Behind Moffee's home was the most colorful garden I had ever seen. There was produce and flowers in abundance. It was beauty and nourishment, enough for the soul and belly. I could not have designed a home any better. After exploring all of Moffee's home, he bid me to walk with him.

By moonlight, we followed a beautiful creek down to the shore of the great lake. Talking as we walked, he suddenly carried on our conversation from the opposite side of the creek. Now how did that happen, I wondered. I hollered across the babbling water, "Moffee, how do I get to the other side?"

Moffee's flower and vegetable garden

He yelled back, "You are on the other side." I didn't quite get it until I saw him sitting on a large boulder laughing loudly with tears in his eyes. After finding a fallen tree on which to cross the creek, we finished our hike to Mono Lake. We sat by the water's edge, listening to it lap on the shore and talked until sunrise. He had much wisdom to share and an answer to everything I inquired about. I couldn't help but ask him, "Where did you acquire such wisdom and knowledge out here in the middle of nature?" With a smile, Moffee said, "All of nature points to where it came from. And where it came from is the author of all wisdom." Moffee also added that when he was young, he learned through many lessons that bad company corrupts good character but if you walk with the wise, you'll grow wise. He continued by saying, "If you don't associate with fools, you'll save yourself from many red faces." My face must've looked obviously puzzled, for Moffee looked at me and explained, "You'll save yourself from embarrassment." "My father," he said, "was my greatest teacher. I also learned much from my dearest friends; some whom you'll meet." Moffee went on to share a wise saying from the father of his close friend Whitey; a proverb that Moffee said he never forgot. He proclaimed, "A fool inherits folly but the wise are crowned with knowledge. The wise also gives thought to their steps." I felt like a most privileged student as my new found mentor looked intently into my eyes and said, "John, you too will learn to speak with wisdom and knowledge. There's plenty of gold and rubies out there, but lips that speak wisely are a rare jewel indeed." Something certainly mysterious is going on here. Moffee speaks as though he knows something about me and my future; something I know nothing of. Time passed without awareness as Moffee's words bubbled from his sweet spirit into the deepest parts of my being.

Sunset on Mono Lake

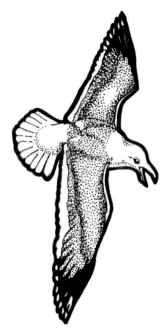

Brine shrimp delivery

Brine shrimp

From one evening to the following sunset, I listened to him celebrate another day. Looking at the brilliant colors of the sky, Moffee excitedly honored his Maker as the best artist of all. He loudly proclaimed, "Ah, behold, the painter of sunrises and sunsets. Because of Him, a sunset can be seen twenty-four hours a day . . . somewhere."

I strolled back to where the sandy shore met the prairie grass. Sitting down, I was content just observing Moffee as he went about his daily routine. Several seagulls swooped down across the lake on a course directly toward him. The birds were attracted to Moffee's high pitched scream which sounded just like a seagull hovering in the wind. They brought him tiny brine shrimp, which apparently had a medicinal value when correctly concocted, . . . so he said. In exchange for these salty tidbits, Moffee would sit there on the shore and groom their feathers. I was most fascinated and impressed with their relationship.

6

Watermelon time

I got a real kick out of a particular observation of Moffee. He was very fond of watermelon. He could quickly devour one in a single sitting. He had the most peculiar habit of aggressively playing with his toes when he was eating his favorite delights or telling stories. Manipulating his toes was a dead give away of his contentment.

It just so happened to be the second Tuesday of the month when, as always, seven of Moffee's close friends would make the trek to visit with him, fellowship and enjoy their monthly soak together,

Dikee

There was "Dikee", a tea trader from the grand valley to the west. You could tell that everyone loved to see him. He would bring the most incredible tasting wild blackberry tea from that big valley of his. It was the most pleasant, almost euphoric drink I've ever sipped. When he wasn't cultivating his tea, he would hike the mountains setting trails only gnomes could see. He created scenic trails to various waterfalls; trails in and out of the valley floor; trails past trees so giant you can't see the tops of them and even a trail to a colossal granite monument he called "Half Rock". Not shy by any means, Dickee made everyone laugh a lot. It certainly was a trait everyone enjoyed.

On the trail to Half Rock

Bodie's home

Then there was "Bodie", a gold prospector from an old abandoned mining town north of the lake. He carried with him a large blue trunk. It sounded as though it was filled with many gold coins. No one ever asked, for this would not be polite. Also in the trunk were various musical instruments which he would play at a moments notice. I believe he must've had the grandest mustache anywhere.

Bodie playing a tune

Beneath each nostril was hair long enough to braid a ponytail. No one built fireplaces or chimneys as well as Bodie could. He would often insert a gold nugget into the middle of his handiwork. It was his signature and trademark. From his trunk, he discreetly pulled out a five stringed instrument he called a belly box and a single drum he played with his foot. By playing a little tune, you could tell that Bodie wanted to get this shin-dig underway. My favorite song he sang was called "Bonnie's Mountain Man". It must have been about a true love of his; for when he sang the chorus, Bodie's eyes glazed with obvious longing and melancholy. He never missed coming down out of the hills for any festive get-together.

Moe – the colormaker

There was "Moe" from a canyon called Lundy. It was a famous place known for its beautiful fall colors. His well-tailored clothes were also brightly colored; like autumn itself. Everyone said Moe was exceptionally gifted with the things of nature. He could walk past an aspen tree in late summer and leaves would turn from old green to early fall colors. Some gave him the nickname "Colormaker". He was especially known throughout the mountain country for his flying skills. He would hold onto the ankles of large birds and steer them to whatever peak he wished to stand on. Ravens were his favorite as they were strong and more agreeable with him. He cherished the fellowship and camaraderie of his dear friends; both birds and little people. Arriving on time, Moe made a perfect two point landing while hanging from one of his ebony winged friends.

Two point landing

Gateway to Horsehoe Canyon

Not far to the southwest, nestled in majestic Horseshoe Canyon, is the little village of "Gnome Hollow". The canyon is known for its pristine alpine lakes where fishing is always superb. From the hollow, three of the small folk always managed to make their way through the pines, along the creek, then on down to Mono Lake. They would be there whether summer or winter. The three would always arrive with something gnomes can't live without, - CHOCOLATE! Without exaggeration, they must've brought a hundred pounds or more in their back-packs. Just before they would head off to Moffee's they would hurriedly go to "Brook's Chocolate Compulsion Shoppe" and purchase an immense amount of the sweet brown stuff. Brook was the finest chocolatologist in Horseshoe Canyon . . . well,

Brook the chocolate lady

Toffee's favorite pastime

she was the only one. Gnomes came from far and wide to sit in her shop. It was a social center for fellowship and of course eating chocolate. The three gnomes spoke most affectionately of her. Brook's husband, Toffee, often helped her make her candies. He is the real master confectionist of toffee and brittle at his wife's shop . . . (thus his nickname).

All gnomes in the canyon are avid fishermen and Toffee is the most avid of all. Everyone wanted to fish with him for his good fortune seemed to permeate everyone around him. With gnomes, fishing is just what one does during ones spare time. And with gnomes, there is never a lack of spare time. According to rumors, Toffee's secret to catching large trout was chumming with chocolate truffles. Toffee's other great passion was fire. There are some who might consider this rather unusual, but he was recognized as the premier campfire builder throughout the Mono Lake Basin gnome country. When any important gnome meetings were called for, Toffee was designated as the one to let all area gnomes know of these assemblies. He would build a great fire and display spectacular smoke signals, which were not only informative but incredibly entertaining. For great distances, a gnome could see one of Toffee's messages in the sky; so all were without excuse from attending any gnome gathering.

Wiz the woodcarver

One of the three gnomes who comes to Moffee's monthly get-together is a famous wood carver called "Wiz"; short for Wizard you know. And surely he is that. He could take a Jeffrey pine burl and magically carve the most wonderful faces and animals of every kind. Somehow he could see things hidden in wood that were waiting just for him to release. Many gnomes had the front doors of their homes artistically designed by Wiz. They were pieces of craftsmanship that belonged in a museum. If a face were carved on a door, it would

speak soft and disarming words to all who would knock. Words that would make the most intimidated stranger feel welcome and at ease. The Wiz was also a highly skilled carpenter. Many gnomes had their quaint little homes crafted by him. During the winter season, many little folk who enjoyed cross-country skiing had their skis ornately carved by this lovable wood wizard.

One of Wiz's door carvings

Quaint little home

Willy the potter

Then there is "Willy"; a potter extraordinaire. If you drink tea, and all gnomes do, chances are your mug was hand formed by Willy. He also created gorgeous vases which were highly prized and sought after. Around the perimeter of these vases, Willy would often paint marshmallow like cumulous clouds with deep, rich glazes. If you looked closely, you could see those clouds changing shape and you could hear wind blowing. If you spoke into his large vases, you could hear the echo of your words seven times over. Other times, if a large vase was asked a serious question, it would answer with great wisdom. Willy always carried a vase with him wherever he went; sometimes for entertainment and sometimes just for directions to help him get where he was going. Willy was often the blunt of a joke for he had a tendency to get lost. This was rare for a gnome.

His smaller vases whistled ethereal-like melodies which could easily set your mind adrift. When I first encountered Willy, he told me to ask his vase any question. With much curiosity I asked, "What is the secret to good health?" It answered "A merry heart does good like medicine." Pulling back quickly, all I could say was "Wow." All the little people responded back with a "Wow" also; first slowly, then with much enthusiasm and laughter. The word "wow" must've sounded odd to them, for they were reacting as though they never heard the expression before. After many questions to the vase, I couldn't help but wonder how such a wise voice could come from this jar of clay.

Whitey the shopkeep

There was a tinkering gnome they called "Whitey". He could fix anything. He was called Whitey for all the hair he had was pure white, like fluorescent snow. He loved to fish, of course, and to smoke his hand-carved hickory pipe filled with blackberry leaves he traded with Dikee for. He is a store-keep in his village. It was a regular occurrence to see a "Gone Fishing" sign on the front door of his shop. With biggies, (outsiders) if one fishes too much, he might be considered lazy. But amongst gnomes, if one doesn't fish, he's considered a bit of a sluggard and a bit irresponsible. Whitey's store was no ordinary store indeed. The things he sold were most unusual. I mean, whoever heard of rainbow trout jelly beans? Or pine cone stew? Or pine nut milk? Or spiced tapioca lemon tufa cookies? Say that three times.

Gone fishing

Whitey's shop

These things certainly never intersected my life's path. It definitely must be a gnome thing. Whitey was very accomplished at bartering. He always carried a small bottle of homemade hot sauce. He would always put exactly three and one half drops in his mug of tea; never more. Many throughout "Gnome Hollow" sought out Whitey for his good and wise counsel.

Sandoo

To round out the group of eight, was the tallest of the little people. His name was Sandoo Sniknedge. I remembered his last name because it was fun to say. His overwhelming smile was extremely contagious. Even though all gnomes laugh a lot, I think he laughed the most. He resided beneath a huge bristlecone pine at the base of a mammoth-sized mountain south of Horseshoe Canyon. Now a bristlecone pine has the distinct reputation of being the oldest living thing on the face of the earth; some almost five thousand years old. Sandoo arrived adorned with a beautiful necklace, bracelet and a spectacular oversized belt buckle; all of which he designed and made. With much respect

from his community, he was called a prince of jewelers. Later that evening, as the sun set behind the mountains, I couldn't help but notice Sandoo's magnificent buckle. On it, he had meticulously engraved a mountain landscape of various colored metals. From one of the sculpted mountains, a golden crescent moon rose and slowly moved across the buckle. As the moon rose, this buckle glowed brighter and brighter lighting up the underside of Sandoo's pudgy belly. Sandoo said that his buckle design enabled him to walk anywhere at night, especially through the forest which was his favorite place for creative inspiration.

Ancient Bristlecone pine

Gnome greeting

After all had arrived at Moffee's home and were greeted most hospitably, they would clasp each others forearms, bow and press the tops of their foreheads together. This obviously was a great sign of respect among gnomes. They then picked up their personal belongings and made their way down to the shore of the great lake. There, by the edge of the lake, they immersed themselves into the prettiest turquoise blue hot water springs I had ever seen. To my amazement, Moffee and his friends allowed me to join them. I felt eager and most honored. As they slowly entered the hot water, they began discussing the more serious issues of the day, but never with unkindness or complaining. I leaned over and quietly spoke a comment to Moffee who was sitting next to me. "I've yet to hear any negativity against anyone or anything. I'm not accustomed to such constant gracious communication, with and without words. Do all little people have this

The monthly soak

refreshing quality?" I asked. With gentle instruction, Moffee said to me, "One who guards his mouth and tongue keeps himself from calamity." Whitey glanced at me and added "Yes John, and a gentle answer turns away wrath but a harsh word stirs up displeasure." Then almost like a three part chorus, Willy adds, "Reckless words pierce like a sword but the tongue of the wise brings healing." How absolutely and delightfully wonderful are the words I'm hearing this day. Again in amazement, I wondered how everyone could join in the answering of my question which I asked Moffee in private. Gnomes must have acute hearing, I thought. Or maybe it's just something else I don't understand.

It took a little while to adjust to the hot water; but in time we all began to relax, soak, suck chocolate, sip blackberry tea, and commence to telling great stories. They were stories so full of visual pictures that they somehow transported me to exactly the places they spoke of. They fondly told the funniest stories of a past mutual friend named Bundee Eegnuts. It sounded as though he must've been their favorite humorist and practical joker. They told of how Bundee would get down on all fours behind a tree and would snort like a bear when friends would pass. Bundee would then lie on the ground laughing as hard as a gnome could laugh. Bundee said that nothing runs faster than a gnome when startled; not man nor beast. Because I could see this story so clearly, I laughed as though I was actually there. I laughed as though I knew him.

This gregarious group of friends would laugh till they cried. They enjoyed each others company immensely. Although discreetly polite, the eight referred to me as an "outsider" or a "biggie". On any other occasion, I might have felt awkward or uncomfortable being referred to as different from the rest. But the little people said it in such a way as to almost make me feel special; like royalty.

It seemed as though the hot water somehow carried me away to another world or dimension. I began enjoying the hot springs and stories way more than I normally would have. There were stories of animals, stories of flying, stories of dark nights, stories of close encounters with outsiders, of hilarious pranks and practical jokes, of enchanting tales of gold, silver and precious stones. And there were great stories of things I could never even imagine. Because of the amount of time spent listening to these great conversations, I knew that by the end of this day I would have a serious case of prune skin. Suddenly, Bodie abruptly jumped up, opened his large blue trunk and grabbed a fiddle. With everyone's eyes fixed on him, he began playing and singing a most haunting, yet delightfully enchanting story and melody. Sitting there in the water, staring at more brilliant stars than I had ever noticed, I could see in the moon's face that it too was enjoying the music and stories. Whatever was happening to me had become a most pleasant experience. Maybe it was the blackberry tea. After mustering a little courage, I spoke up and told one of my favorite stories. I felt confidently excepted when my new friends began laughing. Maybe it was just my face. I wasn't sure. I sensed we were becoming great friends. I couldn't help but wonder how many other "Biggies" had ever experienced this unbelievable dream.

Story time

Whenever Moffee or the other little people would say, "I have a hankerin'," this meant they had a very passionate and serious want. So when someone had a hankerin' for some blackberry tea, he had better get it soon or he might get a little uppity; which really was no big deal at all. Now Moffee always had a hankerin' for watermelon, chocolate tapioca pudding, lemonade, or popcorn and sweet cream; (which by the way, goes well together). Each gnome of course had his own particular hankerin'. But all had a deep hankerin' for music and dancing, sooner or later.

Pretty Breezy

Moffee & Breezy

The last several times that Bodie came down from the north, his sister Breezy came with him. She told her brother it was to help him carry his things; even though a gnome can carry up to three times his own weight. After she and her brother arrived at the gathering, it became quite clear of her intentions. She had eyes for Moffee and he was quite fond of her as well. It was easy to tell, for their cheeks would turn bright red and they would giggle in an odd but most charming manner. She came escorted by her brother for this was the proper thing to do. She always had great respect for her brother's fellowship while he and his friends enjoyed their monthly soak. The hot water had to wait though until Moffee pushed Breezy on a swing he hung from a nearby tree. Romance always comes first among little people. Swinging was almost like meditation to a gnome. My, how those two would giggle as Breezy sailed back and forth to Moffee's gentle push. Their giggle made me laugh. Whenever Breezy came to visit Moffee during the cold winter months, the two of them enjoyed ice skating. Moffee would show off for Breezy as he would gracefully spin and glide across the thick ice. He somehow seemed to skate even beyond his own ability. Ah, the power of love. Female gnomes were especially attracted to male gnomes when they would show off just for them. This was both courtship and flirtation amongst gnomes.

Showing off

Later, while in the hot springs, I respectfully commented to Moffee that he had good taste in ladies. "Breezy is very pretty and seems to have a very sweet heart," I said. He told me that there was much more to her than what a first encounter would tell you. Moffee told me, "There are many in the area who has been the recipient of Breezy's generosity. She opens her arms to those who lack and extends her hands to the needy." I couldn't help but respect Moffee immensely, for he truly looked at the heart of a person and not the outward appearance. He proudly made one more compliment of her by boasting that, "She is clothed with strength and dignity and she laughs at the days to come." His boasting of her was affectionately poetic.

When the gnome men folk were done with their soak and had temporarily exhausted their stories, they emerged from the hot water, dried off and with much anticipation, prepared to return to Moffee's home. As I came up out of the water, my knees were quite wobbly. It must've been a longer soak than I thought. Whitey looked at my shaky knees and said to me, "John, are you all right?" Dikee jokingly interjected, "Yeah John, your eyes look a little glazed. Have you been eating donuts?" Everyone laughed loudly. That was funny. Initially I was a little slow with gnome humor, but I believe I'm getting it . . . well mostly.

When we arrived back to Moffee's home, this company of friends found everything spotlessly tidy as always. His large pinewood table was set for the supper event of the month. Moffee would always say, "And who did this?" He would look at Breezy, knowing full well this was her doing. Then they would turn bright red and commence to giggling. Moffee gently, yet loud enough, slapped his large hand on the table getting everyone's attention. He looked at all his friends, smiled and loudly proclaimed, "Look at Breezy everyone. She watches over the affairs of my household and does not eat the bread of idleness." Embarrassed, Breezy blushed when all the men folk yelled, "Hear, hear!" But it was embarrassment that she happily accepted for she knew that Moffee was showing deep affection and honor for her.

Then all would take hands, give thanks and eagerly dig into large helpings of mushroom steaks smothered in apricot sauce, dandelion and trout fritters, acorn muffins, mashed sweet potatoes dripping with butter, a large assortment of colorful vegetables and of course, blackberry tea. They all ate four or five times more than I ever could. I imagine a meal with a bunch of Vikings would have certain similarities. It was chaotic, boisterous and great fun. It felt like a kid getting desert before dinner. I could not help but think, "If all gnomes eat like this, where do they get their supply of food?" Moffee did it again by answering my thought. "He who works his land will have abundant food, but he who chases daydreams lacks judgment and goes hungry." I did manage to squeeze a piece of fresh hot cinnamon plum crisp, piled high with chocolate chunks into my already overstuffed belly. WOW!

After a most magnificent meal, Moffee and all his friends engulfed Breezy with a very respectful little people hug of appreciation. They dismissed themselves to the soft sofa room where they reclined around the lodge-like fireplace. There they took a twenty-four minute wink nap. I had to take a walk outside for I had never heard such snoring. The entire room felt as though a high speed overhead fan was turned on. After all awoke, they proceeded to tell more stories. The fine meal and snooze seemed to give everyone a second wind. At one point, Moffee turned to Breezy, who looked absolutely beautiful in the firelight and said, "I have a hankerin' to read some poetry." Then Breezy responded, "And I have a hankerin' to cook something sweet and sew you a many colored coat." For these are the things, amongst many others, that women gnomes loved to do for those they cared about. Moffee then read some poetry which he wrote. You could tell where Moffee's inspiration came from for Breezy blushed brightly.

After many days, I think, I began to remember. I remembered I was a "biggy" and this was not my home. For some reason, I can't be certain, I believe I met Moffee on a full moon. Suddenly I realized it was a full moon later. What has happened to me? Then the most amazing memory of all; I remembered and longed for my beloved wife Jilly and our home. I jumped up and quickly, but not rudely, said goodbye to Moffee and the others. They all looked at me as though I would be back soon. "Thank you so much for everything you've taught me," I humbly said to Moffee, "And for all your overwhelming acceptance and generosity. How I will miss you and all my new friends." He took my forearms and we bowed toward each other touching the tops of our foreheads. I had a strange feeling that he passed something special on to me. As I waved goodbye, Moffee imparted one last jewel to me. "John," he said, "You are a generous man and if you continue to give freely, you will gain even more. A generous man refreshes others and will prosper."

Uplifted and encouraged by Moffee's words, I hurried home in the dark. I was certain that Jilly would be waiting for me sick with worry. Had I been under some kind of spell all this time? When I arrived at home, I found her sound asleep cuddled under her favorite quilt. I sat beside her and gently touched her face. She awoke halfway, smiled and said, "Couldn't sleep, huh?" I was extremely puzzled as she showed no worried concern at all. I crawled in bed beside her and deeply fell asleep the remainder of that night. I didn't awake until the crack of noon to the smell of Jilly's coffee. "Yes, I'm home," I thought.

John and Jilly's mountain cabin

Sitting on the porch of our mountain cabin, enjoying coffee and blackberry jam toast, I intently kept my eye on Jilly, waiting for her to ask me where I've been. She never did. She only commented on how blue the sky and lake were. Finally, jumping up, unable to stand it any longer, I rapidly began spilling my adventure with her of Moffee the Mono Gnome. I apologized numerous times throughout my story for not contacting her sooner. With all pleading sincerity, I tried my best to convince her that I had truly lost all sense of time and reality with Moffee Vicket. "Believe me Jilly, something most peculiar happened to me," I said to her. She put her hand on mine and said, "Honey, are you all right?" I think I frightened her with my sincerity. I could tell she was convinced that I believed what I was saying was true. She tried comforting me by telling me that it must have been an amazing dream I had. What she said next stunned me. "You were only out walking two, maybe three hours last night." The toast I was eating fell out of my mouth. I was a bit panicked, but the blackberry jam tasted so familiar.

Several nights later, on the waning side of the moon, I was compelled to take Jilly back with me to the tufa forest on the shores of the great Mono Lake. I had to take her, for the way she looked at me after I told her my story put some serious doubt in my own mind as to the authenticity of my alleged adventure. I know she accompanied me down to the lake just to humor me and help me bring closure to this crazy notion.

We walked right up to the exact tufa I was sure Moffee made his home in. There was no door, no porch, no light, no chimney, no windows, and no garden. "Am I going crazy?" I thought. With much compassion amidst my confusion, Jilly took my hand and said, "Let's go home honey. It has been a beautiful walk." I was numb and began questioning the validity of my sanity.

The next full moon, while asleep under my quilt, I awoke to what I thought was the smell of blackberry tea. "No, no, no!" I muffled to myself. I buried my head under my pillow. After tossing for who knows how long, I surrendered to what I had to do . . . go back to the tufa. I dressed myself and ran.

As I arrived with heart pounding, there was Moffee waiting to greet me. He was most happy to see me and very excited about wanting to share gnome things with me. As we sat in the grass under the bright moonlight, he began sharing secrets of the Mono Gnome and the little people. "Every seven years, we little people choose only one outsider to reveal ourselves to. And if the outsider be married, we reveal ourselves to the two, for the two are one." he said. He told me that gnomes do not show themselves for such a long period of time so that their legend and mystery would remain. "Come back," he told me, "on the next full moon and bring your bride." I wanted to beg him not to trick me because my wife might have me committed to some kind of mind evaluation. I did not ask because I did not want to insult him. He always spoke the truth. Then, in the middle of my thought, he was not there. He was just not there. "Oh, how I hope this insanity doesn't start all over again," I said out loud.

Twenty-eight days had passed like a snail. I persuaded Jilly to take a walk down to Mono Lake on the full moon on which Moffee had invited us. I believe we were both a little reluctant. "Just a walk," I declared to Jilly. I dared not tell her of my last encounter with Moffee; especially of this particular invitation. As we got closer to the tufa towers, I became very anxious and apprehensive. I did not want to feel foolish again. But to my surprise, there in front of us was Moffee's home with the front door wide open. A soft golden orange light glowed through the windows and out from the open door. It seemed to bid us "Come in." I stole a quick glance at Jilly to see if she was seeing what I was seeing. There was no doubt about it. She was finally experiencing what I told her about. Her eyes were as wide as I've ever seen and her smile was of pure enjoyment. I had never seen her face like it before. Pure delight filled her countenance. I couldn't help but wonder what my face looked like the first time I saw Moffee and his home.

Being "biggies", the door appeared way too small for us to enter, just as it did the first time I came here. But we did enter and didn't even have to duck our heads. Once inside, Jilly became completely enthralled with the skilled craftsmanship of Moffee's home. With her delicate hands, I think she touched every carved beam, chair, table, lamp and whatever piece of woodwork she saw. By touching all the carved interior of Moffee's home, Jilly was paying high compliments to all the little people whom she hadn't had the honor of meeting yet. She then became mesmerized, staring intently into the depth of one of Willy's vases; both inside and out. Just as with my first vase encounter, she asked it many questions at my prompting. Jilly carefully asked her first question. "Will I live to be an old woman?" The soft deep voice answered, "A woman is immortal until her work is done." Delightfully satisfied, she boldly asked another. "Will my life be difficult?" Again, the beautiful vessel faithfully answered Jilly, "It will not be sunshine everyday. Sometimes there's wind, clouds and rain. But the sun always comes out again." Jilly turned to me, gave me a tight embrace and with her eyes asked for forgiveness for not believing my story. I squeezed her in return, letting her know that everything

was all right. After all, who could believe such a tale? We both were curiously drawn to the large pinewood table in the middle of the dining area. On this exquisitely carved mass of timber lay a rather large and alluring book. I felt sure it was opened for our eyes to see. The cover was ornate with thick leather, reddish in color. Embossed around the edges were green vines. The pages were a light beige parchment with brown ink and gold leaf calligraphy

The Mono Gnome's most important book

throughout. This book was truly a piece of art in itself. Contained within the pages of this magnificent book was the "Genealogy", "History", "By-Laws" and "Standards to Live By" of the Mono Gnome. I happen to notice in the "By-Laws" section the part where the Mono Gnome reveals himself to an "Outsider" every seven years. The by-law right below that turned out to be most interesting. It said, "And every forty-nine years, (that's 7x7), ye shall pass the torch on to a worthy "Outsider" who shall take thy place to rule over and keep safe all of the creation within thy boundaries appointed unto you." Jilly looked at me with astonishment and said that my beard had grown at least five inches during my reading of the book. The by-law continued on by saying that the present Mono Gnome, Moffee Vicket, shall then become an "Outsider" and live the remainder of his years wherever he chooses. "Your beard grew another three inches and is starting to glow," exclaimed Jilly, "and I believe your ears are getting bigger." Searching the book further, I began reading the genealogy of all the "Mono Gnomes" that went back a thousand full moons. Then all of a sudden my heart leapt to my throat. There, inscribed in brown and gold was my father's name. I knew him as Andy, but as a "Mono Gnome" he was called Bundy Eegnuts. Now things made much more sense to me. I now know why my father knew so much about the gnome legends and in such detail.

Shattering my deep thought, both Jilly and I heard the unmistakable giggle of little people. We hurried to the door and in the full moon light saw Moffee and Breezy dancing hand in hand. Their smiles went from ear to ear in unison. Moffee approached and spoke to us one last time. "If you pursue love and right living, you will find true life, prosperity and honor." He bowed and touched both our foreheads with his. We both had happy tears as Moffee turned and joined his Breezy. They waved and danced off into the outside world together . . . and they were gone. We never saw them again.

Moffee and Breezy waving goodbye

Looking at my beautiful Jilly, it was easily noticeable that her ears had also grown bigger. Then the strangest thing happened to me, for I said to her, "I have a hankerin' for some blackberry tea." She looked at me, called me by a new name and said, "Little John, I have a hankerin' to cook something sweet and sew you a many colored coat." Then with bright red cheeks, we both began to giggle in an odd but most charming manner.

THE END

I would first like to thank God for giving me the wonderful gift of art.

To my wife Jill, for her support, encouragement and editing.

To my children, Bree and Bodie, for their "You can do it, Dad."

To my computer guru, Tobin.

Thank you deeply to all my dear friends who live in or have been to Gnome Hollow.

To my fellow gnome Ron, who dreams with me.

To the staff at Westbow Press.

…And to all the Biggies (Outsiders) who pronounce it Maw-no, instead of Mōnō.

About the Author

John moved to the beautiful Eastern Sierra of California in 1965. He honed his artistic skills as a graphic artist with Standard Oil and Lockheed Aircraft. He owns an art gallery with his wife Jill and his two children Bree and Bodie. He enjoys painting landscapes, playing guitar and fishing.

CPSIA information can be obtained
at www.ICGtesting.com
Printed in the USA
LVIC07n0709230813
349235LV00002BC

* 9 7 8 1 4 4 9 7 9 8 1 6 1 *